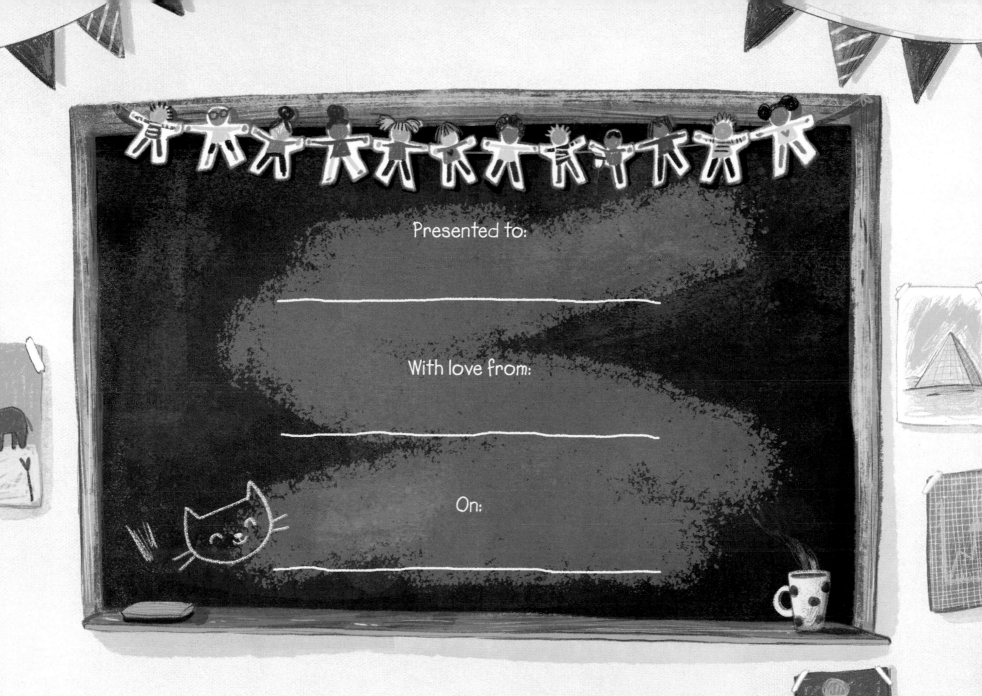

Presented to:

_____

With love from:

_____

On:

_____

ONE BIG HEART full of gratitude to my mom ... for everything!
–LD

For my family near and far,
who love each other just the way they are.
–LF

19 20 21 22 23 / DSC / 21 20 19 18 17 16 15 14 13 12 11 10 9 8 7 6 5 4 3 2 1

One Big Heart

A celebration of being more alike than different

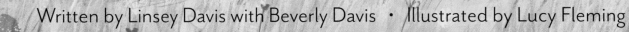

Written by Linsey Davis with Beverly Davis • Illustrated by Lucy Fleming

ZONDERkidz

In one itty, bitty corner of ou[r]
is our teeny, tiny classroo[m]

great, big world,
filled with happy boys and girls.

Star Chart
Amanda
Ayden
Sam
Gracyn
Lauryn
Jaun
Reed
Elle
Well done!

APPLE
starts with

Aa

Each one of us is different,
'cuz what fun would it be
if I looked like my classmates and they all looked like me?

Our faces make a

RAINBOW,

lots of colors all around.
Shades of tan and melon skin
and even chocolate brown!

Some are missing two front teeth,
while others smile with dimples.

God made each of us unique—
it really is that simple.

Some have wavy hair on top,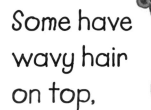

while others wear theirs straight.

Some sport afros, twists, or braids.

Juan is **SHORT** and Reed is TALL. We're every shape and size. Some have freckles on their nose and some have bright **blue eyes.**

God gave us different bodies that can do amazing things.

With one arm Elle does CARTWHEELS

and my friend Amanda sings.

Sam loves telling stories and wants to learn to read.

Noah wears a bright red cape and runs with **SUPER SPEED**.

costumes

Mila plays a princess with a long, pink, ruffly dress.

Asher likes to jump and SPLASH and often makes a MESS.

The bell rings and we head outside for recess in the sun.
Our giggles and our laughter show **we ALL like having fun!**

I see those smiling faces and understand today,
we're more alike than different in many special ways.

We each have rhythm deep inside that makes us want to **move.**

We love to **run** and **jump** around and find our playground groove.

Back inside for music, we **bop** to every beat. We wiggl

…nd *dance* sideways. We **clap** then **STOMP** our feet.

And afterward it's lunchtime—our favorite time of day.
No matter what we choose to eat, our taste buds shout,
"HOORAY!"

Each of us is **CURIOUS**.

We can't wait to explore.
We ask a lot of questions ...

AND THEN WE ASK SOME MORE!

When I
grow up...

Happy ♥

We all like to imagine and let our minds run free
To draw or write or dream about what we'll grow up to be.

We all have great big feelings that don't always stay inside.
Sometimes we've gotten angry. Sometimes we've sat and cried.

Then a friend will cheer us up and fill our lives with joy.
We all need friends who give us hugs or share a favorite toy.

But the way we're most alike ...

the **MOST IMPORTANT PART?**

God gave us all a special gift–

We each have ...

One BIG heart

We've got a lot of elbows.
We've got a lot of hands.
We've got eyes to help us see and feet so we can stand.

But the thing that matters most is something we can't see.
The touch of God that's inside you and also inside me.
That's the place where kindness grows
and where love gets its start ...

Deep down in our
PUMPING
THUMPING
ONE BIG HEART.